Dina Prima
The Ballerina

written by Mary E. Ciesa
illustrated by Ann Gosser

For Orpheus and Artemis Nurches
For Vera Bolen Hutchison

Balboa Press books may be ordered through booksellers or by contacting:

Balboa Press
A Division of Hay House
1663 Liberty Drive
Bloomington, IN 47403
www.balboapress.com
1 (877) 407-4847

Printed in the United States of America.

ISBN: 978-1-4525-8313-6 (sc)
ISBN: 978-1-4525-8314-3 (e)

Library of Congress Control Number: 2013917393

Balboa Press rev. date: 10/25/2013

Dina Prima tumbled out of bed,
tiptoed down the hall,
bounced down the steps,
and twirled into the room.
She had something important to say.

"I want to be a *ballerina*,"
Dina announced.

She believed it with all her heart.

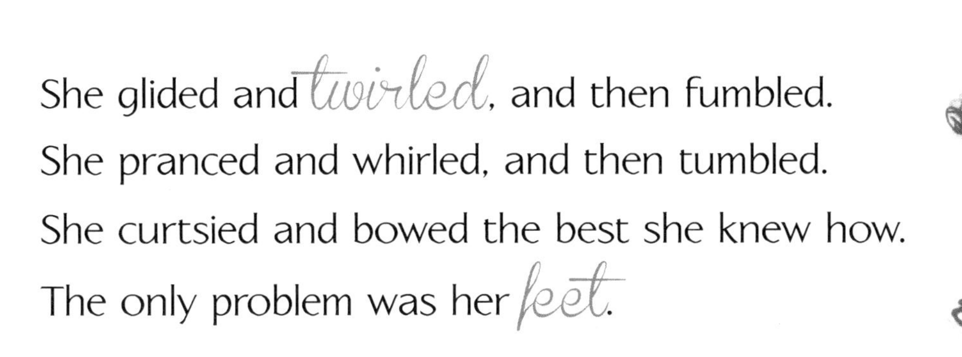

She glided and *twirled*, and then fumbled.
She pranced and whirled, and then tumbled.
She curtsied and bowed the best she knew how.
The only problem was her *feet*.

They turned *in* when they were supposed to turn *out*.

They were always getting in the way.

With a frown, Dina went to talk to her parents.

"Why won't my feet dance like I want them to?"

"You were just born this way, Dina," said her mother sympathetically.

"But it doesn't mean it has to be that way forever," said her father.

"Besides," her mother added, "if you *believe* you will be a ballerina, then you *can* be a ballerina."

Dina smiled.

A glimmer of hope passed through her mind and traveled all the way to her feet.

Mrs. Prima took Dina to the doctor the next day.
The doctor looked at Dina's feet and watched her walk.

"We can easily fix your feet."

"What do you mean?" asked Dina cautiously.

"Special feet need special shoes," said the doctor.

"*Special feet?*" Dina repeated.

"Yes. If you wear orthopedic shoes ..." He paused. "Or shall we call them *special* shoes? If you wear special shoes, your feet will straighten out in a few years."

He wrote a prescription for the shoes, gave it to Dina's mother, and patted Dina on the head.

When the *shoes* were ready, Dina and her mother went to Milton's Shoe Store to pick them up.

"Well, what do you think of your special shoes, young lady?" asked Milton the salesman as he lifted the tissue covering the shoes.

Dina took one look at them, doubled over, and held her stomach.

"Those aren't special shoes," she said firmly. "Those are *ugly* shoes, *especially ugly* shoes!"

The shoes were brown and thick, and they turned out in a very strange way. When Dina put them on and took a step, they made her trip.

“I can’t even go up on my tippy toes,” she whimpered.
“They feel as heavy as cement.
They look like a big mistake.
I hate them!
I hate orthopedic shoes!
I hate special shoes!

I hate ugly shoes!”

When Dina got home, she ran to her bedroom, kicked off the shoes, hid them under her bed, and cried herself to sleep.

That night, she dreamed she was a beautiful *ballerina* dancing across a stage.

In the morning, Dina pretended she couldn't find her shoes. Then she put on her mother's high heels and *snuck* off to school.

Later that morning her mother realized what Dina had done, so she brought the special shoes to school and took her high heels back home.

"Oh, fiddlesticks!" said Dina in a huff.

Dina frowned and put the ugly shoes on.
The rest of the day was not much better.

"Your shoes are on the wrong feet," teased Tanika.

"Brown doesn't go with pink," said Debbie.

"Those are some ugly shoes," said Sandra.

"These are special shoes," said Dina with a quivering lip.
"They're for my special feet. I'm going to be a ballerina."

"Yeah, right," said Sandra. "I'm glad I don't have *special feet*."

Slowly Dina got used to the special shoes.

A day passed, and then a week, and then a month, and then a year, and then another whole year.

Dina's feet slowly *straightened*, just the way the doctor said they would.

Finally it was time to see the doctor.

He looked at Dina's feet and watched her walk.

"Well, will you look at that!" said the doctor. "You're walking as gracefully as a ballerina. In fact, I think ballet lessons may actually help your feet."

"*Yippee!*" Dina jumped and twirled.

On the way home, Mrs. Prima drove by the old mansion up the street. "Miss Grace has a *dance studio* there. It's close to home, and you can walk there by yourself."

"I can't wait!" said Dina.

At last the day came for Dina's first *lesson*.

She kissed her mother good-bye and clip-clopped to the end of her street. She passed the Smith's charming *cottage* and looked for the gray stones that marked the path to the mansion.

The worn
stone path led her
through the English garden.

"Mmm, the flowers smell so good."

Dina *skipped* after a butterfly
and chased it all the way to the side
entrance of the old mansion.

She stood there with her ballet slippers in a bag and stared at the big old *wooden door*.

It groaned when she opened it.

From somewhere high above, she heard the tinkling of music, and she started up the stairs.

Her heavy shoes made the old stairway creak.

Dina opened the dance studio door.

She pulled off the brown shoes, exchanged them for soft, pink leather *ballet slippers*, and wiggled her toes to the ends.

“Excuse me,” she said politely. “Is this where I become a ballerina?”

Dina closed her eyes and imagined her *dream*.

“Yes,” said the dance teacher, Miss Grace. “If you see it, your feet will believe it.”

Miss Grace showed Dina a picture of a real ballet dancer.
Dina smiled.
A glimmer of *hope* passed through her mind and traveled to her feet.

Dina joined the class but *froze* when she saw Sandra, Debbie, and Tanika. They were already at the ballet barre.
Dina's stomach knotted.
The girls giggled when they saw her.

"What is so funny?" asked Miss Grace.

"Dina's feet!" said the girls all at once, pointing.

"Yes, they are *beautiful*, aren't they? Just like a ballerina's," said Miss Grace with a kind twinkle in her eye.

Dina smiled and held her head high.
She straightened her back.
She promenaded to the barre and stood like a perfect dancer.

Week after week Miss Grace noticed how Dina glided and *twirled*, how she pranced and *whirled*, and especially how she curtsied and bowed. Dina's special shoes had made her legs strong and steady.
Her feet turned exactly the right way for a ballerina.
The light ballet slippers made such a difference; it was like she was dancing on a cloud.
One day, Miss Grace announced, "I have chosen Dina to be the prima ballerina in our recital next month. She will be the lead dancer."

The girls moved back so that Dina could be at the front of the line.
"Stand in position with arms and feet," said Miss Grace. "Listen to the music and count the beat. Point your toes; plié just so. One, two, three ... move *gracefully*."

Dina beamed.

She preened.

She felt like a *dream*.

Sandra, Debbie, and Tanika looked at Dina, wanting to be just like her. For weeks they tried to imitate Dina everywhere she went.

They all *slid* down the banister when it was time to go.

They *danced* through the mansion on their tippy toes.

They *peeked* through heavy curtains, pretending to be on stage.

And they *tiptoed* around a bearskin that made them afraid.

They *glided* gently past the big Grecian vase and
practiced their dances with perfect grace.

After weeks of practice they were ready to go and *pirouetted*
to the carriage house for their grand little show.

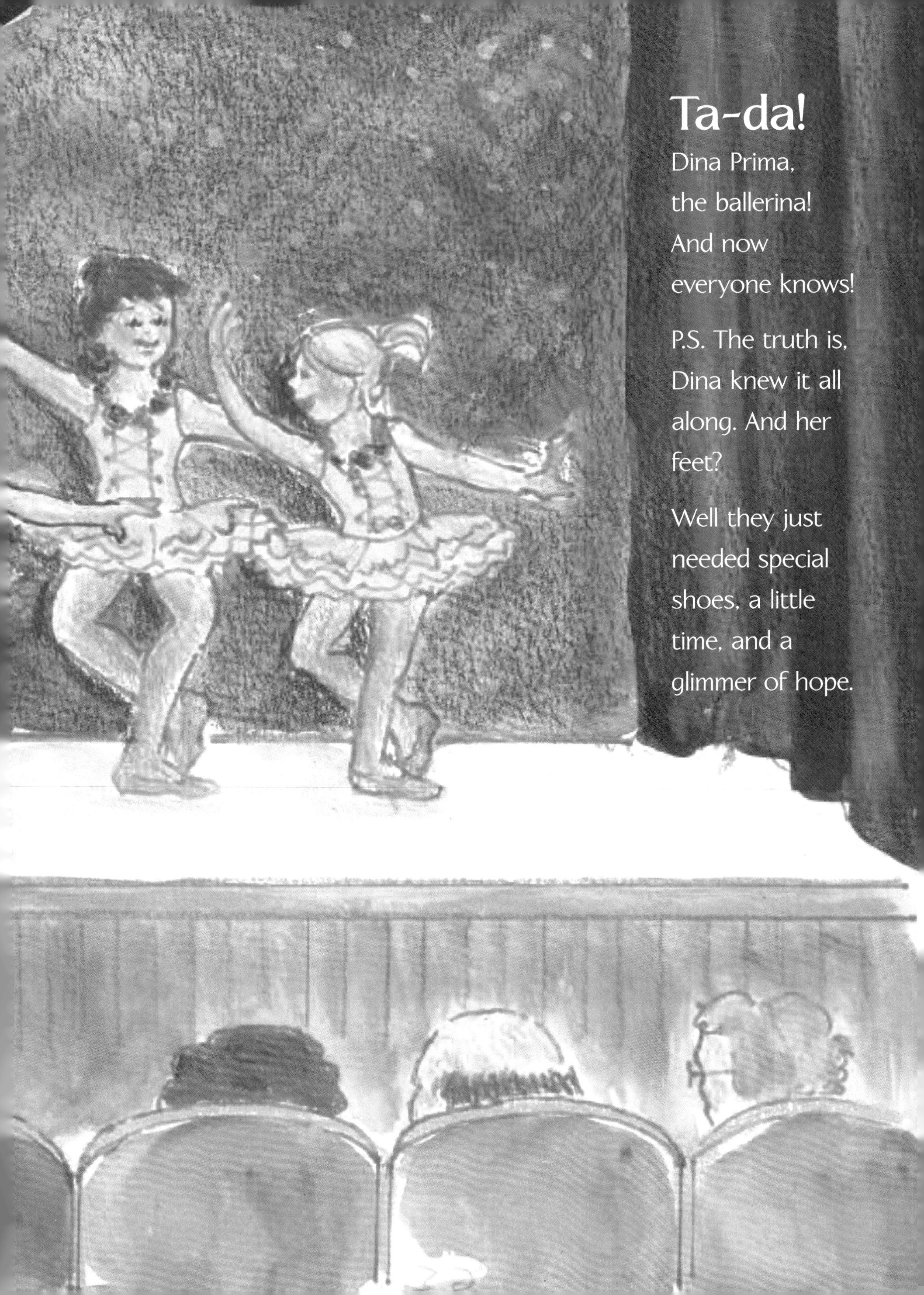

Ta-da!

Dina Prima,
the ballerina!
And now
everyone knows!

P.S. The truth is,
Dina knew it all
along. And her
feet?

Well they just
needed special
shoes, a little
time, and a
glimmer of hope.

Some of the settings and illustrations in *Dina Prima the Ballerina* depict the real Tudor Revival country estate, Stan Hywet (pronounced hee-wet), in Akron, Ohio. Now on the National Register of Historic Places, Stan Hywet was once the home of F.A. Seiberling, founder of the Goodyear Tire & Rubber Company, and his family.

When mother and daughter (Verna Bolen Hutchison and Ann Hutchison Gosser, the illustrator) wanted to find a place to give ballet lessons, they discovered a room in the Stan Hywet Manor House that was perfect for a dance studio. They rented the room and provided Russian ballet lessons for children in the surrounding area.

Mary Nurches Ciesa, the author of the book in your hands, was one such child. She lived in the neighborhood behind the Stan Hywet Manor House on Courtleigh Drive, the same street as the Smith's charming cottage. The Smith's cottage was once home to Stan Hywet's poultry man and is also on the National Register of Historic Places.

The author and illustrator gratefully acknowledge the assistance of Stan Hywet Hall & Gardens in Akron, Ohio.

Author *Mary Ciesa* had the magical experience of taking ballet lessons in the Stan Hywet Manor House as a child. Now a member of SCBWI (Society of Children's Book Writers and Illustrators), a nurse practitioner, and a Zumba® instructor, Mary still believes in the power of hope.

Illustrator *Ann Gosser* is a professional freelance artist specializing in illustrating, mural painting and fabric art.

CPSIA information can be obtained at www.ICGtesting.com
Printed in the USA
BVIW12n1219180215
388206BV00002B/2